What a Girl Wants

What a Girl Wants
Beauty ♥ Health ♥ Happiness

Karen Cooper
Illustrated by Mei Lim

Scholastic Inc.

New York   Toronto   London   Auckland   Sydney

Mexico City   New Delhi   Hong Kong   Buenos Aires

Before using any of the health and beauty recipes in this book, first test a little on your skin or hair.

No part of this publication may be reproduced in whole or in part, or stored in a retrieval system, or transmitted in any form or by any means, electronic, mechanical, photocopying, recording, or otherwise, without written permission of the publisher. For information regarding permission, write to The Chicken House, 2 Palmer Street, Frome, Somerset BA11 1DS, United Kingdom.

ISBN 0-439-29638-2

12 11 10 9 8 7 6 5 4 3 2   1 2 3 4 5 6/0

Printed in the U.S.A.   40
First Scholastic printing, July 2001

CONTENTS

INTRODUCTION

Hooray! As a girl, you've got a whole lot to be excited about (. . . OK, being one, I could be a little biased). But for real, today's girls can do anything — from sports to shopping, science quizzes to sleepover parties, and everything in between! Yet even with all the zillions of great opportunities out there, there's still the annoying stuff like zits, boy issues, and friendship fiascos that go hand in hand with growing up. But never fear, *What a Girl Wants* is here! After all, your trip (and it is a trip) toward teenhood should be as fun, fulfilling, and totally fabulous as possible! Want to find out the best way to cope with a major crush (and still manage to show your face in public)? How to deal when your best friend doesn't turn out to be exactly the best? If you can actually avoid those horrible bad hair days? *What a Girl Wants* will tell it like it is, from the real deal on relationships to health and beauty tips and beyond. Check out advice from girls, do-it-yourself recipes that totally work, major dos and don'ts, and tons more! So to find out how to make the most of the wonderfully unique, fully fabulous girl that YOU (and only you) are . . .

PART 1
RELATIONSHIPS 101

When it comes down to it, even more than clothes, even more than your autographed Britney Spears CD, relationships are supremely important. If you think about it, we have relationships with lots of people: our parents, our sister or brother, friends, teachers . . . even the cute guy who takes your order at the pizza place. (OK, maybe he doesn't think it's a relationship, but it might be in your mind!) When our relationships are good, a lot of other stuff falls into place easier — it's not as hard to brush off a bad day and good days can be all that much better!

As girls, we want to "connect" with people and **EXPRESS** ourselves! There's nothing better than having someone fully understand who you are inside and out . . . and still want to spend time with you! Which is great . . . otherwise we'd be going through life like a bunch of unfeeling robots just moving around each other. Sure, as a robot you wouldn't feel the pain of being completely ignored by a crush, or of getting a D on a test. But you'd never have that intense feeling, like when your mother agrees to buy you that new top from the Gap that you've been dying for because you did some extra stuff around the house. Or when that special guy totally makes eye contact with you in math class, and you even manage to say something funny. That rocks!

But when things aren't 100 percent with those you care about, it can be a total drag. Maybe you're fighting with your sis because she ruined your favorite shoes, or your "best" friend decided to buddy up with someone else, or your parents just grounded you for not doing your chores without giving you a chance to explain. Yeah, sometimes it can feel like the world is against you. The good news is that no matter how bad things look at the moment

... NOTHING IS FOREVER ...

So if you've had a fight with a friend or a not-so-great phone convo with a crush, instead of "instant replaying" over and over in your mind (as we girls can do so well) and making the problem into an international crisis, there are things you can do to avoid, fix, and get over the problem — and get on with all the great things you should be doing! Remember: Practice makes perfect!

Chapter 1

Self-image:
I Like Myself . . . I Think

I Like Me for Me

You've heard it before, but I'm going to say it again and again and again. . . . (Yep, it's that important!) Before anyone can like you, you have to like yourself. Seems pretty obvious, right? Well, sometimes it's not that easy. Puberty is knocking at your door and your body is changing. Your emotions can go a little haywire at times — something as small as a zit might be enough to make you want to hide under your pillow all day. Well, zit or no zit, you are **AMAZING!**

Picture yourself as an individually wrapped gift. No matter how the outside is decorated (with ornate bows or newspaper!), it's what's inside that's really interesting! There is no one else in this wide, wide world who's "packaged" with the exact same combination of thoughts, feelings, talents, likes, and dislikes as you. And what's great is not only finding those around you who share some of these same qualities, but appreciating and learning from the differences you find in others when you untie the bow. After all, how **B-O-R-I-N-G** would life be if we all looked and acted the same?! You can bet that shopping would not be half as much fun if we all wore the exact same clothes. And why would you bother having a conversation with somebody if you already knew what she was going to say? It's the differences in people that make life so interesting. So make the most of the individual YOU are and help make the world a more exciting place!

There's usually one song that you listen to and feel totally alive and like "yourself". . . whenever I find myself losing touch with who I am I just turn on that song in my head!

LAURA, 13

Be True to You

Odds are you probably like who you are inside but sometimes worry that others won't.

Rule #1: Make sure that the person the world sees is YOU! Some people may pretend to be someone they're not because that's who they think others will like. While it may get them a few superficial "friends," in the long run, it's the REAL friends who know and like the REAL you who are worth having (plus, who wants to spend all of that time and energy having to "act" like someone she's not?!). Might sound a little corny, but the most important relationship is the one you have with yourself, so be true to you! If you don't have a good relationship with yourself, it's pretty tough to have a good relationship with anyone else. Most people like spending time with those who are happy, confident, and secure with themselves. A few don't, but it's probably because they are a) jealous, b) insecure, c) totally lack your "I rock!" attitude, or d) all of the above. And if someone doesn't appreciate you for you, it might seem like the end of the world at the time, but there's no shortage of other (and probably better) people who will!

SELF-IMAGE

13

It's important to remember that everyone's under the same pressures to like and be liked as you are. Best way to do it? Like the song goes, "You've got to be real!"

> The secret to being comfortable anywhere, anytime, with any group of people: Be comfortable with yourself.

When you're down on yourself, you kind of know, or hope, that you'll fit in somewhere, sometime. And you do – you just have to hang in there. But before then it hurts if you let it get to you.
EDEN, 14

Who am I? In order to like yourself, you need to know yourself! Right now you're probably learning lots of things about **YOU** . . . what kind of music you're into, what sports you're good at, what style clothes you like, what kind of books you enjoy reading. There're lots of ways to discover who you are!

Journals are great (if you can remember to write in them and keep them out of the **Write it!**

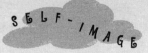

reach of your little brother!). Putting your thoughts and feelings down on paper can definitely help give you a clearer picture of how you feel about certain things. If you think about it, it's sort of like talking to yourself without worrying about people thinking you're crazy! You can write about how nervous you are about giving that oral report next week, how intense it was to score the winning goal in yesterday's soccer game, how cute the guy is who sits next to you in English . . . anything that's on your mind is up for grabs!

Do-It-Yourself Journal — Make It Even More Personal

A journal is a wonderful and personal thing. But you can make it even more personal by creating your own customized journal. You can go to an arts & crafts or department store and pick up a blank notebook. Decorate the cover with pictures, post-cards, ribbon, fabric . . . anything that says "YOU." You can also poke a small hole in the spine and tie an end of a ribbon through and knot it. Let the rest of the ribbon hang inside the book for a place keeper!

Make a Personality Collage!

Instead of tossing out those old mags and catalogs,

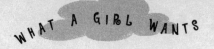

flip through them and cut out the pictures you like. Pick out things that appeal to you . . . photos, sayings, fun illustrations, poems, comics . . . anything that touches you: heart, mind, and soul! Paste them onto a piece of cardboard and presto! Your own personality collage!

· ·

Top 10 Lists

These are also a great way to get to know yourself. You can use them to get a journal started or as a fun activity to do with a friend! Here are some topic ideas, but you can totally make up your own, too!

· ·

Top 10 Things:

· · . that I like to do when I'm by myself

· · . that I like to do with my family

· · . I would like to learn how to do

· · . that I'm good at

· · . that I absolutely adore

· · . that I totally can't stand

This is one I did for fun!

....

Top 10 Things That I Like to Do with My Friends:

1. *Chat on the phone*

2. *Shop, shop, and shop*

3. *Take a kickboxing class*

4. *Gush about our latest crushes*

5. *Share our favorite books*

6. *Go to the beach*

7. *Have dance parties on the living room couches*

8. *Visit new places*

9. *Make jewelry*

10. *Check out basketball games*

Get Involved!

The more you get to know yourself, the more you can get involved in the things that interest you. Not sure if you'd like horseback riding or pottery lessons? Give new activities a try and find out . . . you never know! Finding things you feel strongly about not only helps you feel good about yourself, it gives you the chance to meet people who like to do the same things!

Emotional Rescue

No matter how confident, secure, smart, pretty, fun, or athletic you are, there are going to be those not-so-great days that happen to everyone. Maybe you got partnered with the boy of your dreams in science lab and accidentally burned his favorite jacket with the Bunsen burner. Or maybe your Spanish teacher asked "How are you" and you thought you were responding "Fine, thank you" in Spanish when you were actually saying "You smell like a cow" and the whole class erupted in hysterics (except for your teacher). Yep, the important thing to remember is that we all do and say stupid things — so take it easy on yourself!

Next time you have a bad day (and we all do),

instead of convincing yourself you're the biggest loser on the face of the earth and refusing to show your face outside of your bedroom, think of all the things you are good at, the people who like you for you, and all the good things that you do. Whether it's your mother, father, sister, teacher, best friend, or dog, it's important to have someone you can turn to when you're not feeling so great about yourself — to remind you how wonderful you really are. Just call them your "support system"!

When things aren't going the way we'd like, it's easy to get so wrapped up in the problems that we can forget about everyone else. This really doesn't get you anywhere. In fact, the best way to get out of a funk is to do something good for someone else! Not only will you make that person happy, but you'll feel good about yourself, too! Give it a try!

Smile Power! Best way to turn that frown upside down? Start smiling! Studies have shown that just making yourself smile can actually put you in a better mood!

Chapter 2
Friendship:
The Good, The Bad . . .

Girlfriends are the greatest! After all, who else can you share your deepest secrets with and know she won't tell anyone? Who else will split that huge chocolate sundae with you when you're feeling down? Who else can make you laugh until your stomach hurts? Don't get me wrong, no one

can beat the kind of love we share with our families. But after our families, the most important relationships in our lives are with our friends. We have a different kind of relationship with our friends. Maybe it's because we're born into our families and they're always there for us, while we have to choose our friends ourselves. And when things with our friends are going great, nothing could be better. At the same time there's nothing worse than losing a friend. So how do we make friends, and more important . . . keep them?

Making Friends

Girls are everywhere! In your history class, in your neighborhood, at ballet lessons, in school clubs, on your soccer team . . . everywhere!

So how do you become friends with them?

Think about the way you became friends with the girlfriends you have now. You probably started talking to each other and found out that you had common interests — maybe you liked the same band, wore the same style clothes, enjoyed the same activities. Everyone wants to have more friends.

The key is finding friends who you like spending time with and who you can trust.

Say "hi" to someone new every day . . . it'll make them and you feel great!

Making Friends: Dos and Don'ts

Do be friendly but not desperate!

Don't talk about yourself all the time.

Do ask them questions about themselves, but don't pry into personal things.

Don't rush things, a friendship takes time to grow.

Do develop the habit of looking cheerful and happy.

I have two best friends, one is Rianne and the other is Chanda. Chanda is cool to talk with – we don't really play. Rianne and I like to play and ride bikes. I like them both for different reasons.

MARISSA, 11

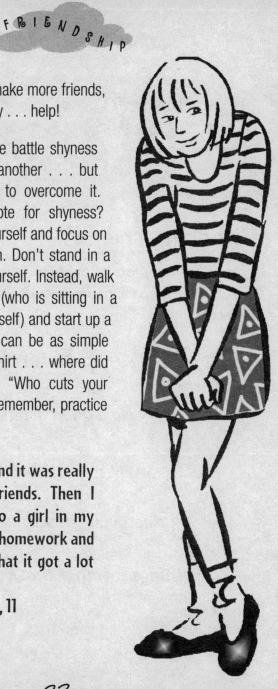

Q. I'd like to make more friends, but I'm really shy . . . help!

A. Most people battle shyness at one time or another . . . but there are ways to overcome it. The best antidote for shyness? Forget about yourself and focus on the other person. Don't stand in a corner all by yourself. Instead, walk up to someone (who is sitting in a corner all by herself) and start up a conversation! It can be as simple as "I like your shirt . . . where did you get it?" or "Who cuts your hair, I love it!" Remember, practice makes perfect!

I used to be shy and it was really hard to make friends. Then I started talking to a girl in my math class about homework and stuff, and after that it got a lot easier.

ELLIE, 11

People love hearing their own name! When you're talking to a friend (or potential friend), use her name often . . . it's guaranteed to make her feel special!

Keeping Friends

Sure, there're lots of opportunities to make friends, but once you've made friends, how do you keep them?

Ways to Keep Friends

Be a good listener.

Keep your promises.

Keep your friends' secrets.

Do things together that you both like.

Be kind.

24

Just as there are tried and true ways to keep friends, there are equally surefire ways to lose them. Here is a list of things to definitely avoid in a friendship.

Ways to Lose Friends

Talk about her behind her back.

Blab about her most personal secrets.

Tell her crush how much she likes him (without her permission).

Always cancel your plans or show up late.

Forget to call.

Leave her out when you're around another friend.

Use her to get something you want.

Being a good conversationalist means being a good listener! Ask people questions about themselves. People love talking about themselves and what they're into.

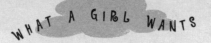

I like my friend Myiesha because she makes me laugh
and we act goofy together!
MARY, 10

Don't be a know-it-all . . . it's a total
turnoff!

To become and stay good friends you need to gain
each other's trust. That means keeping your
promises, being true to your friendship, and honest
with each other. A trusting friendship doesn't happen overnight, though. You have to earn trust little
by little. You share, she shares, you share more, she
shares more. Each time you "connect," you get a
bit closer. Eventually you learn if this is a person
you can trust . . . or not.

I remember that I was out of school for a couple of
weeks. When I came back two of my friends had suddenly become like best friends and were working on a
class project together. They totally left me out when
I came back and I had no one to work on the project
with. The next week a new girl came in to school and
we became partners. She and I are still best friends
and the other two girls aren't even talking to each
other anymore!
BETH, 11

The Popularity Trap

For many people, being "popular" means being a part of a "clique" or in with the "in crowd." Guess what? Popular really means being yourself and being able to get along with a lot of different kinds of people. It means you're liked because of who you are, your talents, your personality, your sense of humor, your kindness . . . whatever. Being your own person is the way to go . . . it's more impressive than wearing the same clothes as the "in crowd," hanging out at the same places, and doing the same things they do.

Really, who wants to be a total copycat? The key is to find a group of people who you enjoy hanging out with, whether they're part of the "in crowd" or not.

I have lots of friends and we all treat each other nice. I think that's important. I wouldn't want to hang around together if we were mean to each other.
CHRISTINE, 10

If you're friendly and nice and genuinely yourself to everyone, people will definitely take notice — and want to check you out! Having confidence in yourself totally attracts others to you. (This does NOT mean being a snob . . . in fact, most snobs are

insecure, that's why they have to ACT like they have all the confidence in the world.) The key (again) is to be **REAL**!

Just a simple smile and "hi" can make others want to get to know you.

Be nice to everyone. Studies show (OK, informal studies with my friends) that those guys and girls who are so ultrapopular at school aren't necessarily the ones who turn out the happiest, most successful, or fulfilled. It's those who are more consistently nice to everyone who end up ahead in the end!

A Little Secret

It may come as some surprise, but kids in the "in crowd" don't have as many **REAL** friends as you may think. "Getting in" to a clique is never easy, and a lot of girls fear losing their "place" once they've been accepted — and can do some pretty mean things to make sure they keep that "place." Imagine not being able to trust anyone because they might backstab you and try to ruin your rep, just to "secure" their position in the group! Who needs that? You're way better off being nice to everyone and having **REAL** friends who you can trust!

Chapter 3

Oh, Boy! What's the Big Deal Anyway?

As a girl you probably have a definite feeling about boys . . . whether those feelings are positive or negative is a different story! You might find yourself wondering: Why do they act so weird? Why does he totally bug me? And if he bugs me so

much, why can't I stop thinking about him? If you're lucky you might already have some friends who are boys and get along with them just fine. Congrats! But it's not always that easy. Maybe boys totally annoy you . . . or maybe you're starting to realize that they're not so "icky" after all. Either way, they can seem like a totally puzzling force that might just as well come from another planet. Well, the truth is, girls and boys are different . . . but that doesn't mean you have to spend your entire lives on opposite sides of the playground.

First (and probably most obvious) are the physical differences between girls and boys. You've probably heard that girls "mature" faster. So what does that mean? Well, it's likely that you're probably taller than a lot of boys in your class. Girls tend to grow faster on the outside, and on the inside, too. You might find that you and your girlfriends started

30

to read faster, for example. This is just the way nature works!

Other differences might not be so obvious. These aren't because boys and girls are different when they are born. Both boys and girls pretty much come into the world with the same basic wants and needs . . . a big one being relationships. And while girls continue to put an important focus on relationships, boys are taught (by television, the movies, video games, and the people around them)

to be strong, tough, independent. Have you ever heard "You throw like a girl" (although with some of the girls I know, that would be considered a compliment!). Or "Boys don't cry"? Kids learn how to act from all kinds of things — from the toys that parents buy them (what if girls always played with trucks . . . and boys with Barbies?) to the colors boys and girls wear as babies. (Why don't girls wear blue and boys pink?) This is called socialization and sometimes it can help us get along in the world, but sometimes it can keep us from being who we feel we are on the outside. Sometimes it's hard for boys to develop close relationships because they're taught to hide their feelings and be "tough." You're lucky to be alive during a time when these roles are changing

and girls are allowed to be strong and boys can show their feelings and still be "tough." The first step in understanding each other and narrowing the gap is to get to know each other as friends and learn how each other really is on the inside! Don't try to turn boys into you with your way of thinking . . . but share interests. Best way? . . . Friends first!

Getting to Know Him

While most boys might not be up for a marathon clothes buying trip at the mall or getting together to do your nails or a face mask, and maybe they can't understand why you're sobbing over the latest Julia Roberts movie, they can still make great friends and open up new activities and different ways of looking at things that you might not have otherwise discovered!

Sure, getting to be friends with a boy may sound easy. But what's the best way to do it? First, just like being friends with girls, don't pretend to be someone you're not! Falseness will not get you far. Second, be interested in hearing about the things he's doing. You might want to ask him:

1. How his football/baseball team is doing. You might even want to consider checking out one of his games with some friends. (Just don't giggle and point at him the whole time!)

2. To a party! Have a bunch of his friends and your friends over for an afternoon of fun activities everyone would enjoy . . . pizza, softball. (Save the face masks for the gals!)

3. To work on a home-work assignment together — or study for a test.

OH, BOY!

I'm friends with some boys in my classes. I never really think about whether they're boys or girls . . . they're just fun.

ALISA, 10

The Crush Question

It happens. You're walking to class and your eyes lock (OK, maybe they just meet for a fleeting instant) with that new boy in your English class.

Your heart starts beating faster, your hands get sweaty, you feel like you're going to throw up if you don't see him . . . and throw up if you do! Is it a sickness? No, it's a crush!

Having a crush is pretty much like being on a roller-coaster ride. One minute you feel like you're floating on air because he said "hi" to you in the hall and the next minute you're, well, crushed, because he didn't even notice you in the school lunch line. But before you send your best buddy snooping around to find out if he feels the same way, first find out whether he's crushworthy or not.

Does he pass the crush test?

Does he:

- Treat his friends well?

- Like animals?

- Hang out with nice people?

- Laugh at your jokes?

- Say "please" and "thank you"?

Who wouldn't want to spend time with a guy who's caring, fun, and respectful? This guy sounds like a sweetheart. Good choice!

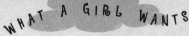

Or does he:

Always goof off in class?

Come to school late more often than on time?

Make fun of people?

Keep not-so-great company?

Swear, smoke, or steal?

Run, and run as fast and far away from him as you can . . . now! This guy may try to appear like Mr. Cool, but you're better off warming up to someone else!

Crush Dos and Don'ts

Don't ever put anything in a note to him that you wouldn't want the rest of the world to see (because they might).

Don't call him twelve times a day . . . he (and his parents) will probably get really annoyed.

Do smile and say hi when you happen to see him in the hall.

Don't follow him from class to class hoping to "bump" into him.

Do try to get to know him as friends first.

And most important . . . DO have your own life!

He Likes You. Now What?

The moment you have been daydreaming about (instead of doing your homework, chores, or practicing the clarinet, etc.) for weeks has finally happened. Your BFF just found out from your crush's best friend who sits next to her in math class that your crush likes you! Holy macaroni! Now what?

This can be a little nerve-racking . . . for both of you. What happens when you see him in the hall? Do you approach him or should you wait for him to do something? Should you write him a note or call him? Suddenly you go from complete bliss to pretty much wanting to throw up.

It's normal to feel awkward or scared. Finding out someone shares your "affections" brings up lots of questions: Will we have to kiss . . . what if I don't know how?

Does this mean we have to talk on the phone every night? There aren't any hard and fast rules . . . it's basically doing what you feel comfortable with. Odds are if you both enjoyed hanging out before and have stuff in common, the butterflies will go away. If it's right it will feel right . . . just keep checking in with yourself and make sure you are comfortable with how things are going. And if you feel more comfortable getting to know him better as a friend first . . . tell him! He might be a little hurt . . . or a lot relieved. Being friends first can take lots of the pressure off. And if he doesn't want to wait around for the friendship thing he's not the guy for you. There will be others . . . promise!

41

Lots of times girls will feel pressured to "go out" with a boy because they want to impress their friends or prove that they can "get" a boyfriend. These aren't great reasons. Make sure you're doing what you're doing for YOU and not someone else!

"I Like Her as a Friend"

So you're counting the seconds until you meet your BFF after school with the news you've been waiting for . . . does he like you or not. You're imagining all the fun things you'll do together, what it will be like to hold hands with that boy of your dreams . . . then the news hits. He "likes you as a friend." Yep, this news can be crushing, especially when you've been making up fantasy dates in your head. But instead of ignoring him, talking about him behind his back, and buying a voodoo doll with his name on it, you'll come across feeling and look-ing much better if you ACCEPT it with a little bit of grace. Sure, you might get in a good cry for what you thought "could have been" (which might not have even been the case anyway), but then get over it! If he likes you as a friend . . . be his friend. Things happen for strange reasons . . . who knows, the best date of your preteen life could be right around the corner . . . but it won't find you if you're at home sulking under your pillow!

Dating Dos and Don'ts

So you (and your parents) have decided you're ready to start dating. Here're a few ground rules to keep in mind as you head out for the big event:

Don't talk nonstop about yourself (especially the way you look). This is a definite turnoff!

Do ask him about himself — what sports he likes, where he's been on vacation, what his favorite TV show, video game, CD is.

Don't constantly worry about how the date is going, just have fun and relax!

Do be yourself — if he doesn't like it he's not the one for you.

Don't pretend to be someone you're not.

Boyfriend vs.

So things are working out with that special guy, and you're thrilled . . . but your best buddy isn't. Sure, it's great to have a new guy in your life, but be sure not to forget those friends who were there long before him. It's important to make as much time for your friends as you do for your guy. After all, things might not work out with him . . . and if they don't you'll need those friends more than ever!

Love Disconnection

You're convinced he's the love of your life. You share notes, go out for ice cream, and suddenly, out of the blue, he calls it quits.

Yep, it's gonna hurt. The best thing to do is get it out of your system . . . and find someone else! Check in with that support system we talked about earlier . . . they'll help you realize how wonderful, smart, funny, and amazing you are. Remember . . . it's his loss! So instead of crying every night and listening to sappy songs on the radio, go out with

Girlfriends

your friends, take up a new hobby, and feel good about you! Remember, if he doesn't recognize your good qualities, he's not worth it . . . and there WILL be someone who does.

Q&As

Q. How do I know if I am ready to date?

A. This is a decision for both you and your parents to make. If it's OK with your folks and you feel comfortable spending more time with that special guy . . . you can give it a try. And remember, dating doesn't always mean a one-on-one date to the movies. It can be hanging out with a group of friends, doing homework, playing video games . . . just doing it together!

Chapter 4
Family: Survival Skills

Family. You love them more than anything else in the world. You absolutely, positively couldn't live without them. Then how come sometimes they can drive you so completely bonkers?

It's actually pretty simple. You're at a point where you're growing up and starting to think, feel, and have opinions for yourself . . . and sometimes those opinions don't necessarily match those of your family. But don't worry if you don't live a Brady Bunch existence. The truth is, no one does (not even the Bradys)! Every family (just like every person) is unique, with their own little quirks . . . that sometimes you might find fun . . . and some-times . . . well, not. While it's hard to guarantee a stress-free family life through the upcoming teenage years, there are definitely things that you can do to make the ride a little less bumpy. And always remember that as nuts as they can make you . . . it's usually because they love you and want what's best for you!

The Parent Trap

It's Friday night and a bunch of your friends are going to the mall . . . but your mother says no with that most famous parent reason of all time, "Because I said so." You shout, you cry, you stomp into your room, mope, and wonder why life is so unfair. Sound familiar?

It may be the most unjust, unspoken rule of all, but there is no committee, no law, no **NOTHING** that requires parents to give their kids a reason for their actions. (Remember, you, too, will have this power when you're a parent.) But in the meantime it can be super-frustrating if you're the kid. So what's the best way to deal when you and your parents aren't seeing eye-to-eye?

Well, your best bet on what **NOT** to do is not to stomp, scream, mope, and lock yourself in your room. There's probably not much you can do to change their mind, and this is only going to get you upset and lose you some major credibility with the folks. Lie low, read a mag, do your nails, talk on the phone with another friend about how annoying life can be sometimes . . . or even spend time with your brother or sister . . . Eek! Then, the next day, when things have calmed down a little, ask your parents if you could **TALK** to them. In as

calm a manner as possible, let them know how important it is to you to spend time with your friends, how you feel left out when you don't, and ask if there's anything you can do to help build their trust. Taking on extra responsibilities around the house (without having to be asked!), showing that you can keep curfew, getting your homework done, keeping your grades up, and generally being a good kid are just a few ways to earn your parents' trust and respect. Your parents will appreciate you approaching them in such a "grown-up" fashion, and by taking on grown-up responsibilities you may show them that you can handle certain social activities. Good luck!

My mother is really strict. I wish she would trust me more. She always says it's not me she doesn't trust, but other people. It drives me crazy!
ALEXANDRA, 11

Now, more than ever, you're conscious about how other people see you and what they think of you . . . it's one of those annoying things that comes with the teen territory. And let's face it, good or bad, our parents can definitely be a reflection on ourselves. Most kids on the cusp of teenhood tend to have issues with the embarrassing things parents can do. (If you don't, be psyched that you have such cool parents or that you have the maturity to realize that it really doesn't matter!) Believe it or not, your parents usually don't go out of their way to embarrass you, but nonetheless, it can happen. There are pretty much two options: 1. Wear a Buffy the Vampire Slayer disguise every time you step out of the house with them or 2. Get over it . . . it happens to almost everyone.

Top 10 Ways Parents Embarrass You:

1. Wear clothes that are so 1980s.

2. Talk to strangers in the grocery line about YOUR personal life.

3. Say totally corny things in front of you and ALL your friends.

4. Make you dance with your cousin (who's a foot shorter than you) at family weddings.

5.   Hold hands in public and act all mushy.

6.   Listen to the "soft rock" station on the radio.

7.   Point out your "developing" body in front of other family members.

8. *Make you wear the sweater Aunt Edna knit you with the sleeves that are two feet too long.*

9. *Talk about your zit-popping tactics in public.*

10. *Make you take your younger brother with you to the mall with your friends!*

On the Flip Side

As much as our family can make us nutty, you can't find a better support system when you're feeling down. While friends can be fickle at times, you can pretty much be sure your family won't make fun of you, talk behind your back, or spill your secrets to someone else. They're pretty much happy to lend a listening ear 24/7. So next time you get a bad grade on a test that you really studied hard for or find out that the boy of your dreams has a crush on your best friend, go home and have a cup of hot chocolate and watch a movie with the fam! And your family will definitely appreciate feeling needed, too!

Sibling Affairs

Siblings are funny. Sometimes they can be your best friend and sometimes they can bug the heck out of you. Even though you love your brother(s) and/or sister(s) it doesn't mean you're always going to get along with them. You can bet there will be fights over hair spray, clothes, and makeup. Or maybe your little brother will drive you crazy with his tattling and spying on you and your friends. And older siblings love to turn their younger brothers or sisters into personal butlers and maids. (Be kind if you're the oldest!) But if you think about it, no one else in the world shares as much with you biologically, environmentally, and maybe even emotionally! Whether you get along perfectly with your brother or sister now or you have a tough time being in the same room, your relationship will come to mean even more as you get older . . . so get a head start and try your best to get along with them now!

If you're having a major sibling issue that doesn't seem to go away, you might need some parental intervention. Once again, instead of yelling and screaming about your sibling's annoying antics, calmly (the key here is calmly) approach your parents about the problem. Explain the situation and

how you feel. Hopefully your parents can get the two of you together and lay down some ground rules that work out the best for both of you!

Q. I feel like my parents are always harder on me than on my sister. Do they just love her more than me?

A. Just like you and your sister are different, your parents have different expectations for each of you and treat you both in individual ways. Parents love their kids equally . . . sometimes just differently!

Always have fights over who gets what half when it comes to goodies? For total fairness do the "split and pick" trick. One sibling can split and the other picks!

Splits, Steps, and New Families

Families come in all different shapes and sizes. There are single-parent homes, dual-parent homes, stepparents, stepsiblings . . . you name it. And no one type of family is "better" or "worse" or loves their children more or less than another type of family. Not all parents stay or even ever get married. They may decide to split up for many reasons, but mainly because they can't be happy staying together. This does not mean that they don't love you! Actually, many parents split up because they want their children to grow up in a place where the family is happy. Still it can be really, really hard, because your family has changed, and change isn't always easy.

Change brings with it a lot of questions. What will happen to me? My parents? Where will we live? Will they still love me? Will I have to get used to a new family? New friends? The most important thing is to know that you're not alone. Lots and lots and lots of kids go through the same confusion. You might experience anger, hurt, fear, guilt — and all those feelings are completely normal. The worst thing to do is keep all these feelings bottled up inside. You might consider talking to an adult, school counselor, or even a friend who you trust. You may even consider joining a group for kids whose parents are going through a split. You can ask your school counselor or your church to recommend such a program. It can really help when you feel like you're not the only one going through this challenging time. It can be hard for a while, but with enough time and support, things can and do turn out OK . . . sometimes even better than they were before the split.

PART 2
BEAUTY &
STYLE BASICS

Beauty: Inside Out

News flash! Yes, beauty really does come from within! When you feel good about yourself, happiness and confidence shine through! Combine that with eating right, getting lots of rest, exercise, and a good skin care regime, and you'll feel great on the inside and look your absolute best on the outside.

Yep, makeup is a definite blast, and you can't beat finding that perfect hairstyle or a totally groovy dress, but these things should reflect who you are . . . not change it!

So to find out how to make the most of that beauty that already exists — check it out. . . .

Chapter 1
Bad Hair Begone!

Imagine what it would be like if there were no more bad hair days. Just think of how much free time you'd have getting ready in the morning and how much money you'd save on hair care

products . . . ohhh, the freedom! Well, unless you decide to go the wig route (definitely not recommended) or there's some major advancement in hair care technology, odds are that every day isn't

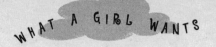

going be a good hair day. But don't worry, there are definitely things you can do to fight the frizz, add some volume, cast some shine, and more. Plus, emergency tactics to try when absolutely nothing else seems to work!

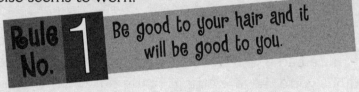

Rule No. 1 Be good to your hair and it will be good to you.

The most important thing in guaranteeing a good hair day is keeping your hair in the best condition possible.

Eat Right and Exercise!

When it comes to food, if you eat junk or just plain don't eat enough, it shows. Hair can become lack-

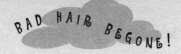
luster and dull . . . or in extreme cases, even fall out! When you nourish yourself you nourish your hair, too . . . so keep up the balanced diet. Chomp on those fruits and veggies and don't forget the water!

Jog your way to lovely locks! Exercising increases circulation, which makes sure your scalp is getting the blood flow it needs to grow healthy, lustrous hair! So get on the running shoes!

Bead-a-rific Hair String

Want to add some instant pizazz to your hair? Try making the latest in groovy locks . . . hair string! Just take a piece of string roughly the length of your hair,

knot one end, and fill with beads of your choice. Knot the other end and stitch to a tiny piece of velcro. Stick the end with the velcro in your hair near the roots and let the rest of the string hang. Totally hip!

Cleansing

Unless you have very oily hair, skip a day between washing. Overwashing can strip your hair of its essential oils and leave it dull and totally hard to deal with. Sure, lots of shampoo bottles say to repeat if necessary (my opinion is that they just want you to use up the shampoo more quickly so you have to buy more!) . . . anyway, one washing should definitely do it.

To Condition or Not to Condition?

The answer to that question is "condition" . . . but the amount of conditioner you use and how long you leave it in depends on your hair type. And remember to give yourself a shot of cold water at the end; not only

will it wake you up, but it will leave your hair look-
ing ultrashiny, too!

Oily Hair

If your hair is fine and/or tends to be on the oily
side, go easy on the conditioner.
Shoulder-length hair usually requires a dollop the size of a dime.
(Adjust accordingly.) Go light at
the roots and concentrate the
majority of the conditioner on
the ends. Leave on for the mini-
mum time suggested (usually a
minute or so) and rinse, rinse, rinse! The key here
is balance . . . too much conditioner on for too long
can totally weigh down hair and too little can make
it tough to manage. Try a little experimentation
with the amounts and you'll get it right!

Do-It-Yourself Protein Conditioner for Oily Hair

Beat one egg white until foamy. Add five tablespoons of plain yogurt. Apply to shampooed,
towel-dried hair in small sections at a time. Leave
in for fifteen minutes. Rinse.

Dry Hair

Dry hair can frizz easily and lead to split-end city. This type of hair requires some more intensive conditioning. Work at least a quarter-size amount through shoulder-length hair from roots to ends and leave on the maximum time recommended (or even a little longer).

✳ After styling, rub some conditioner (just a dab) onto your hands and run through dry hair for total frizz relief!

Do–It–Yourself Hot Oil Treatment for Dry Hair

Place a half cup olive oil and a half cup boiling water into a large glass bottle or jar with a lid. Wrap a towel around the bottle to avoid burning yourself. Shake well until the oil dissolves into the water. Add a few drops of your favorite essential oil (optional). Massage into hair (careful not to

burn your head!). Put a shower cap over your hair and wrap your head in a hot towel that has been soaked in hot water and wrung out. Leave in for thirty minutes, then shampoo as normal.

Normal Hair

Lucky you! You can pretty much maintain your happy locks by washing and conditioning regularly, no special "tricks" necessary! But it's still a good idea to deep condition once a month to promote total shine and bounce!

Do–It–Yourself Mayonnaise Conditioner for Normal Hair

After shampooing, rinse and towel dry hair. Apply one or two tablespoons (depending on length of your hair) of regular mayonnaise to your hair and massage in. Leave in for ten to fifteen minutes. Shampoo again lightly and rinse with a solution of apple cider vinegar and water.

If your hair has been under the constant attack of blow-dryers and curling or crimping irons (which can make ends even more dry and brittle), concentrate an extra amount of conditioner on the ends. And remember: regular trims are a must to combat split ends!

Rule No. 2

Don't fight (too hard) what you have!

When it comes to hair, it seems like it's always a case of the grass being greener on the other side. If you've got curly hair, you wish it were straight; if it's brunette you want blonde, if it's thick you wish you could thin it out. The good news is that there are things you can do to make the most of what you were born with (and this doesn't always mean totally changing it!).

A couple of highlights might be OK, but try not to stray too far from your natural color . . . it's what best matches your skin tone and eye color!

Turn Up the Volume!

Are you always on the lookout for some extra poof? Do you get your hair styled just right, then the minute you walk out the door, it goes limp? Welcome to the world of flat hair. While lots of models and actresses 'try hard to get this "look," many of us who have it would sometimes be happy to trade it in. Good news is that after years of intense, informal research with other flat hair friends . . . the necessary actions have become clear.

1. Try one of the tons of volume-enhancing shampoos out there (always a good bet). Go light on the conditioner (see Oily Hair, page 63) and rinse completely!

2. Totally towel dry! Hair should be slightly damp before adding products and blow-drying, not sopping wet!

3. Rub a small amount of volumizing gel into your hands, rub through the roots of your hair, then comb.

4. Blow your way to volume! Blow-dry your hair upside down to lift your hair away from the scalp and make it "poof" more or use a round brush with a metal barrel to grab the hair near the roots while drying for the same effect.

After blow-drying, I spray some hair spray onto the palm of my hands, then flip my hair upside down and rub it into my roots. When I flip my hair back up, it's like instant volume!

KATELYNN, 12

Straight and Shiny

Have a little more wave than you're looking for? Before you go to the salon or try an at-home chemical straightener, check out these easy (and less costly and less damaging) tips below!

 Shampoo as normal and hit the conditioner hard! Rinse quickly.

 Lightly towel dry.

 Apply one of the great straightening balms that are out there from roots to end and comb through and through and through!

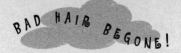
 Get a round metal-barrel brush and grab the underside of hair, starting at the roots. Work the brush from your roots straight down to the ends with your blow-dryer following all the way. Keep doing this until that section of hair is dry and straight. Repeat over whole head.

 Apply a small amount of the straightener to your hands and run lightly over the top of your hair.

Presto! Straight locks with lots of shine!

I have long, naturally wavy hair. When I try to straighten it with a blow-dryer, my arms get totally tired, so I ask my mother or sis for help!
MADELEINE, 11

Cool Curls

Curls, oh, glorious curls! To maximize those bouncing curls you were born with or create waves of your own, here's some surefire advice to get the ringlets you're looking for!

Shampoo and condition as usual. (Use more conditioner if your hair tends to frizz.)

Apply some styling gel throughout your hair (roots to ends).

69

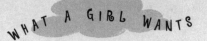
Blow-dry your hair while scrunching it with your fingers.

Voilà . . . wave-a-licious!

For even more curls, try wrapping a section of hair around a large-barrel curling iron. Leave on until your hair is heated through. Slide out the iron and spray . . . don't brush! Finger comb for ravishing ringlets.

If you're a naturally straight-haired person determined to have curly locks, do a test run with the curling iron. If you're sure you like it, take a picture and bring it to a stylist for that more permanent solution . . . a perm! But remember, once it's done, it's done!

Q&A: A Poodle Do!

Q. I got a perm about six months ago and really liked it. Now I've decided to go back to straight and am growing it out. The problem is that I have flat hair at the top of my head and look like a poodle from the ears down . . . help!

ALANA, 12

A. Your best bet is to get regular trims to cut out the perm and cut down on any frizzy ends that can make hair poof even more. In the meantime, try adding volume at the roots (to balance out the look) with some volumizing gel while applying straightener over the ends of hair. Work a round-barrel metal brush through hair from roots to ends, section by section, while applying heat from a blow-dryer. It may take a little work, but this will give you the look you're ultimately going for . . . sans the "flat top"!

Q&A: Avoid Product Overload!

Q. No matter what I do, my hair is always flat. I use lots of gel, mousse, and hair spray, but it still doesn't help. What else can I do?

A. The key here is "less is more"! Try cutting back to just gel and hair spray. And use the gel sparingly and only at the roots! Too many products or too much of any one product can totally weigh hair down and make it stringy and unmanageable. Just a little gel and hair spray will give you the bounce you need!

Bump Up the Color

The coolest thing to come out lately are those hair color wands and color-enhancing shampoos. The best bet is to stay away from permanent hair color. (When women color it's often because they want to regain the color of their youth!) But coloring can get pricey, is tough (and messy) to do at home and get the results you want, plus you're stuck having to deal with those roots!

Instead you might want to try those color-enhancing shampoos for an allover color infusion, or hair highlighting wands to add some pizazz every once in a while.

 To get rid of buildup and boost up that shine, after shampooing, try rinsing with a capful of white vinegar followed by cold water. (Don't worry, it won't smell once you style!)

Flyaway Freedom

Flyaways can plague everyone, especially during the winter when the air can be dry and cold. Make sure you're using conditioner to appropriately moisturize your hair. If after blow-drying you're still having a hair-raising experience, try spraying a little

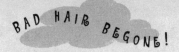

hair spray on a brush and brushing through your hair. Should be smooth sailing from there!

Whenever my hair is full of static, I take the lotion left on my hands after moisturizing and rub it over the top layer of my hair. The static disappears!
SARA, 13

Dandruff Relief

Noticing a few white flakes . . . and it's the middle of July? Time to check out dandruff shampoo! Most of these shampoos you only have to use once a week to keep flakes in check. Dandruff comes from a dry scalp and excess product buildup. So make sure you drink lots of water to keep skin and scalp hydrated and once a week give your hair a vinegar rinse to clean out all the buildup that may have collected!

Dandruff Rinse

Boil five heaping tablespoons of dried thyme in two cups of water for ten minutes. Strain and cool. Pour half the mixture over clean, damp hair. Massage into scalp, do not rinse. Style as usual. (Use second half of solution another day!)

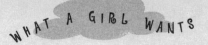

Fast Fixes

Even when you do everything right, you can still have those fluke not-so-great hair days. Here are some great quick fixes to get you out the door looking good in no time flat. (Did I say "flat"? . . . I meant "no time at all"!)

Beautiful Braids

The old standby has some great new twists. Try two low braids, one on each side of your head.

Ponytail Power

Try one low ponytail at the back of your head. Wrap a section of hair around the elastic and secure the end inside the elastic for an ultracool look.

Headband: Great for long or short hair! Get yourself a groovy headband, pull your hair back, and put your best face forward!

Bandanna: One idea that's totally hip is the bandanna trick. Fold the bandanna into a triangle. Put the point toward the back of your head and tie the two front ends behind your ears. For dressier days, try a pretty patterned scarf or kerchief! *Très* cool for long or short locks!

Style It: The Long and Short of It!

Let's make this easy. People love to make rules for who should wear long hair and who should wear short hair. Fact is, anyone can wear either as long as her hair is healthy and she has the right cut. (Just look how many times models and movie stars change their look!)

Find a Style for You

Wouldn't it be great if you could see what your hair would look like with a new haircut before you cut it? Well, you can! Check out www.clairol.com! You can submit a photo (scan it or send it in), then superimpose one of the cool styles they have on file on top of your picture. What will they think of next?!

Fun Stuff

It's party time and you're feeling a little braver than usual. Why not try one of these cute looks just for fun?!

Short Hair: Twist and Spike!

Apply gel to dry hair. Take a small section of hair and back comb so hair is standing straight up, then twist. Repeat all over head, twisting in different directions. Sooooo cool!

Medium Hair: A New twist!

Take sections of hair on either side of your face and twist, gathering more hair as you work toward the back. Fasten in the back with a clip or elastic!

Long Hair: Retro Ponytail

Pull hair back into a high ponytail. Curl bottom of ponytail under with curlers or a curling iron. Totally retro!

Make Your Own Hip Hair Accessory!

Is there anything more hip than wearing your hair in a deep side part with one of those groovy glitter barrettes? Find out how easy (and inexpensive) it is to make your own! (They also make great gifts for friends!)

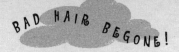

Glitter Barrette

You need: large flat-edged bobby pin

Glue gun or superglue

Flat-backed mini-rhinestones (from a craft store)

Just dab some glue on the outside edge of bobby pin (watch your fingers).

Stick on one of the rhinestones (flat, unshiny side down). Continue dabbing on glue and placing on rhinestones in a row until you fill up the whole side. Allow to dry for one hour before wearing. Try mixing colors and combinations for extra fun!

Beaded Hair Elastic

Remember those beaded bracelets that were so big not so long ago? Turn them into ponytail holders for the latest in hair accessories!

Chapter 2

Serious Skin (and Body) Care

So now you've got great hair, but what about that not-so-attractive red bump that just popped up on the end of your nose? Welcome to skincare 101! But before you read any further, drink a big glass of water (you'll find out why in a little bit)!

Face Facts

When it comes to caring for your skin, it's a good idea to first determine what "type" of skin you have. The options might not be all that exciting, but knowing which you have will help you figure out how to make the most of it!

Oily

Ever feel like your face alone could prevent a major national oil crisis? You're not alone. Odds are if you have oily skin you pretty much know it. It's totally common among girls —

as your hormone levels change your body naturally produces more oil. But if you're not sure, blot your nose with a piece of tissue. If it leaves a major grease mark . . . welcome to the world of oily skin. And it might not be too much consolation now, but way down the road you might be less likely to get wrinkles!

Q. I have really oily skin, so I don't need to moisturize, right?

A. Water-based moisturizer is still a good idea (check out the ingredients), particularly if you have break-out-prone skin. It helps calm and soothe irritations.

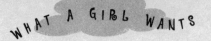

Oatmeal and Apple Mask for Oily Skin

Mix half cup cooked oatmeal, one egg white, one tablespoon lemon juice, and half cup mashed apple into a smooth paste. Apply to your face and wait fifteen minutes. Rinse and pat dry.

Dry

Does your skin flake? Feel tight? You might be overwashing, or your cleanser might be too strong. Use a mild cleanser and moisturizer after washing your face while it's still damp. And drink water, water, water!

Honey Moisture Mask for Dry Skin

Mix two tablespoons honey with two teaspoons milk, smooth over face and throat. Leave on ten minutes. Rinse with warm water.

Normal

Lucky, lucky gal you are! Mild cleanser and moisturizer are pretty much all you need to maintain your balanced skin. But for an extra healthy glow, try this cucumber avocado mask once a week!

Cucumber Avocado Mask for Normal Skin

Combine half cup chopped cucumber, half cup chopped avocado, one egg white, and two teaspoons powdered milk in a blender until they form a smooth paste. Apply to face in a circular upward motion and leave on for thirty minutes. Rinse and pat dry.

To Exfoliate or Not to Exfoliate

No matter what skin type you have, it's always a good idea to exfoliate. Exfoliation is a gentle abrasion on the surface of the skin that clears away dry skin and dead cells — leaving your pores clearer and skin shinier.

If you're using a washcloth on your face, you are already exfoliating.

Do-It-Yourself Exfoliator

Mix one tablespoon honey with two tablespoons finely ground almonds and half teaspoon lemon juice. Rub gently into face. Rinse off with warm water.

Zit Attack!

With the hormone roller coaster ride going on in your body, zits are likely to make an appearance. No matter what you call them, pimples, blemishes, bumps . . . they're a drag. You're producing more hormones, hormones produce more oil, more oil produces zits. Not only can they affect your face, they can affect your self-confidence, too.

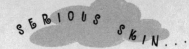

What Not to Do

OK, we've all heard a million times not to squeeze our zits. But sometimes our fingers get the best of us. Here's a guide to when and when not to touch: If it's red, don't even think about it. If it turns a lovely whitish/yellow, then and only then can you consider touching it. But (and this is a super-big "but"), wrap a washcloth around your index fingers and gently apply pressure at the base of the blemish. **DO NOT** use your nails — a guarantee for ugly scarring! Once it pops, dab it with a little hydrogen peroxide to keep it free from bacteria and apply some moisturizer to speed healing.

The Food Connection

Doctors have been going back and forth over this question pretty much since the universe began. (It's kinda like which came first, the chicken or the egg?) Some say to stay away from chocolate, salt, and/or caffeine because they know it triggers "eruptions"! Some people are just more sensitive to foods than others. Best bet: If you eat something and your skin breaks out . . . stay away!

The Toothpaste Myth

Some beauty magazines may tell you to apply a dab of toothpaste to a zit to make it vanish. While it may help decrease the size somewhat, it will also leave a dry, irritated patch that looks even worse!

Blemish Dos and Don'ts

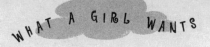

Do . . .

Drink eight+ glasses of water every day.

Moisturize with an oil-free moisturizer.

Wash your face before going to bed.

Use a mild benzoyl peroxide lotion.

Don't . . .

Squeeze your zits.

Touch you face (your fingers can leave bacteria that can cause break outs).

Overwash your face — it can lead to excess drying and irritation.

Get too much sun . . . it increases oil production . . . and zits!

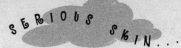

Try This Homemade Pimple Remedy!

Put two or three teaspoons of dried basil leaves into one cup of boiling water. Steep for ten to twenty minutes. Cool and apply to affected area with a cotton ball.

Q. My friend Kate has awesome skin. I use the same stuff she uses to wash my face, but mine still breaks out. How come?

A. Unfortunately, we don't all have the same skin type. Genes, diet, stress levels, environmental factors all play a role. You need to experiment and find the best routine for you!

No matter what you try, still can't get rid of that zit? Check out the section on concealers in the next chapter.

Bogus Blackheads

Q. For the most part, my skin is clear, but I have tons of ugly blackheads. How can I get rid of them?

A. Don't squeeze! This will only enlarge pores and encourage more bacteria and oil to form!

Instead, try this scrub: Mix four tablespoons plain yogurt with two tablespoons grated orange peel. Massage mixture into face for three minutes. (Careful not to get near your eyes!) This recipe will help rid the skin of oil, grease, and dead skin cells — and it smells yummy, too!

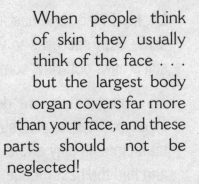

When people think of skin they usually think of the face . . . but the largest body organ covers far more than your face, and these parts should not be neglected!

Body Smooth

To keep the skin on your arms and legs as smooth as possible, try applying baby oil right after you shower! The oil will lock in the moisture and keep your skin as soft as a baby's bottom!

Sun Smarts

The sun is out, it's time to hit the beach . . . but too much sun can lead to a nasty sunburn, not to mention wrinkles and the possibility of skin cancer down the road.

Our friends "down under" in Australia know how to protect themselves from those sun rays.

Follow the Aussie motto:

"Slip, slap, and slop . . ."

Slip on a shirt, slap on a hat, and slop on some sunblock!

Somehow still managed to get too much sun? Ouch! Try an oatmeal/aloe bath treatment. Pour a packet of instant oatmeal into the tub and soak for at least fifteen minutes. Pat yourself dry, then apply pure aloe gel wherever it stings! Aaah . . . total relief!

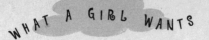

"Water-resistant" sunscreens only remain on wet skin for forty minutes, while "waterproof" sunscreens typically stay on the skin for eighty minutes while you are in the water.

Just Fake It!

Self-tanning cream is the best! Say good-bye to those orangey, streaky self-tanners of yesterday and hello to today's tanners that leave you with a totally natural-looking glow. It's easy! Shower and exfoliate your skin with a washcloth. Dry yourself completely. Before you start application, wet a facecloth and put it aside . . . this will be important later on. Apply self-tanner, starting with your feet and working up. Be careful to pay extra attention to your ankles, knees, and elbows. To avoid tanning your palms, rub the dampened washcloth between your hands. . . . Washing your hands completely will wash the tanner off the back of your hands. This way they stay bronzed!

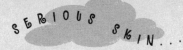

Water Power!

No matter what skin type you have, drinking lots of water is a must! Yep, the stuff that flows freely from your faucet (or bottle, as the case may be) has more power than you think. Water is a natural "purifier," which means that it cleans your body (including your skin) of unhealthy "toxins" (pollution, etc.).

 To keep that glowing complexion all year round, mix a little self-tanner with your moisturizer!

Chapter 3
Makeup and More

Since the beginning of time women (and girls!) have decorated themselves with colorful dyes, powders, and paints as both a means of self-expression and cultural identification. For many of us today, it's still a way to express ourselves, but apart from that, makeup can just be a lot of fun! Experimenting with all those glosses, shadows,

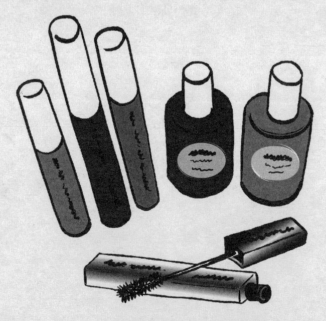

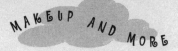

sticks, and creams . . . what a blast! But the number one rule when it comes to cosmetic success is . . . **LESS IS TOTALLY MORE**! Sure, once in a while it's fun to get all glammed up for a big party, but on a day-to-day basis, you're better off not going over-board. After all, you don't want to mask that gorgeous face of yours but make the most of it! (Can you think of anything more icky than that horrid foundation line that makes your face and neck two different colors? Or that awful ring of lip liner that circles the lips of many makeup ama-teurs?) The best compliment you can get when you show your face to the world? "Wow, how do you look so great . . . without even wearing any makeup?!" Let them think it's 100 percent of your natural beauty shin-ing through! (Shhhh! It's our secret!)

As a makeup "artist" you need to prepare your "canvas": Make sure you start with a clean, moisturized face. (Otherwise you run the risk of trapping dirt and oil under your skin and totally clogging your pores, which can lead to major break outs.)

Concealers

Concealer can be a girl's best friend – especially when hormones are bouncing around and those occasional zits seem to keep popping up. Concealers usually come in cream, wand, or stick form. Getting the right color is key. If you can visit a makeup counter in a department store where they match the concealer to your skin, that's great. Apply a test to the side of your face and it should disappear into your skin. If you can't get to a makeup counter, no big deal! Many drugstores let you test it out and take it back if it's the wrong color. You also might consider getting two shades . . . one slightly lighter than your skin and one slightly darker and mixing them together to get just the right shade!

Use a Q-tip to apply a small amount of concealer directly on the blemish. Lightly tap the area with your ring finger to blend. You want the concealer to disappear into your skin rather than sit on top of it.

Powder Power

Powder is great for reducing the "greasies" (especially in that shiny T-zone area on your forehead, nose, and chin) and to set concealer. Once you cover a blemish with concealer, lightly dust a translucent powder over the entire face with a brush or powder puff. Make sure you use a light touch and apply the powder in a downward and outward motion. An upward motion raises those almost invisible hairs on your face, making them stand up and look fuzzy!

Remember: The only thing that looks worse than a big red zit in the middle of your face is a big red zit covered in cakey makeup that doesn't match your skin tone!

The Eyes Have It

They say that the first feature people notice in others are the eyes. So whether you've got those baby blues or are a beautiful brown-eyed girl (or some lovely shade in between!), here are some groovy tips to totally maximize your eyes!

Shadow Secrets

A sheer shimmery neutral color can give you that extra pizazz for a special occasion . . . but stay away from shadow for everyday wear. Think about it: If you're glammed-up every day, there won't be a difference for special occasions! Shadow comes most commonly in powder form, but there are also shadow sticks and shadow creams.

Starting at the inside corner of your eyes, sweep a light, sheer shadow across the lid to the outside corner under your brow. For a little more definition, use a slightly darker color in the crease of your lid and outside of your eye.

Blue eyes never wear blue eyeshadow.

Liner

Eyeliner is a great way to define your eyes and make them "pop" . . . but beware of raccoon eyes!

Powder vs. Pencil

With eyeliner it's ultra-important to go for the natural look. You **DON'T** want a visible line scrawled across your eyelid! If you use a traditional pencil-type liner, hold your eyelid taut with your nondrawing hand. Starting at the inside corner of your eyelid, draw a thin line just above your top lashes across to the outside corner of your eye. Now here's the most important step . . . blend, blend, blend! Using the tip of your finger, gently smudge the line across your eyelid so the color blends into the skin.

For a more natural look, try using a powder liner or eyeshadow to line your eyes. Take a thin makeup brush and wet the tip. Dip it in a dark brown shade of eyeshadow until the brush is coated. Carefully draw a "line" across your eyelid similar to above. No need to blend — the powder gives a softer and more natural look.

Try a dark brown liner rather than black for a more natural look!

Cool tool: Eyelash curlers do what they say — curl your lashes, which helps make eyes look bigger. Place the curler around your lashes and gently squeeze, holding the curler against your eyelid for about ten seconds.

(Just make sure no one is around to scare you . . . otherwise you might have lashless eyes!). Always curl before, NOT AFTER, applying mascara.

Luscious Lashes

If you are going to use just one cosmetic on your eyes, mascara is the way to go. Just a few sweeps of the wand can define, intensify, and brighten eyes! But always put mascara on last if you're using other eye makeup (liners, shadows, etc.), otherwise you're sure to smudge!

Looking in a mirror, start at the base of your top lashes and work up and outward to coat lashes. Do a couple of quick strokes on the bottom lashes, starting at the base as well. To get rid of any unsightly clumps or to unstick stuck-together lashes, use an eyelash comb!

You can use black mascara unless you're super fair-haired and light-skinned. Then go for a brown shade.

Eyebrow Maintenance

Have a few straggling hairs? Think before you pluck! Overplucked brows can make you look like a Barbie wannabe. Just follow your natural brow line and get rid of any excess hair beyond or between the brows. To ease the discomfort, try icing your brows beforehand with an ice cube to numb the pain.

Are your eyebrows a little unruly? Keep them in place with a little hair gel! Just dab a little on each eyebrow and use an eyebrow brush to brush them into place. Presto . . . perfect brows!

Lip Service

You chat with them, you smile with them, and who knows, someday you might even smooch that special boy with them. Here are some great tips for keeping those lips simply smooth and smashing!

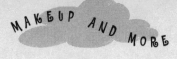

Lip Prep

Got chapped, dry lips? Before you apply any kind of lip gloss, stain, stick, or otherwise, you need to start with a smooth, healthy kisser! For total lip relief, lightly exfoliate chapped lips with a paste made of baking soda and water. Gently rub the concoction against your lips with your finger for about a minute . . . and presto! . . . no more flakes! Pat dry and apply a coat of lip balm.

For severely chapped lips, apply some pure aloe vera gel and vitamin E oil to your lips, then coat with a layer of lip balm to lock in the healing power!

Lip Reference

Gloss: A thick, slightly gloopy, semi-sheer lip cover that makes lips shine, shine, shine!

Stain: Not as thick as a gloss, a stain is a semitransparent covering that gives just a hint of color. The natural-looking way to go!

Lipstick: The old standby comes in matte (no shine) or shine finishes, among others. Lipsticks offer a more opaque cover. (Watch out, too much can leave your kisser looking like a clown's!)

Application

Start with a lip liner that matches or is slightly darker than your lip shade. Draw a line around the inside edge of your lips, starting at one corner of your upper lip and tracing around your lip line to the other corner. Repeat for bottom lip, staying away from the corners of your mouth . . . the top and bottom lines should not meet! Fill in the inside of your lips, using the lip liner to prevent a ring being left behind when your lipstick wears off. Use the tip of your finger to smudge and soften the line.

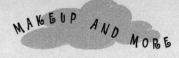
Time to apply! Apply lip color with lip brush (or finger!), starting at the middle and working out.

Blot it! Take a single layer of tissue and gently press lips against it to blot.

Tah-dah . . . totally luscious lips!

 Dot a little gloss in the center of your lips for a fuller-looking pout.

Choosing a Lip Color

Lip color chart

Here are some guidelines for choosing the right lip color for your skin tone.

Fair skin: Sheer, light pinks look fabulous on fair-skinned beauties. Stay away from hot pinks . . . too overpowering!

Medium skin: "Warm" pinks with brown undertones work best on medium skin tones.

Olive/yellow skin: Deep berries and rich rose colors are the way to go. Avoid pale pinks!

Dark skin: Medium and soft, sheer pinks are most flattering. Berries and deep roses also work well.

Natural redhead: Pinks are tough for redheads. Try ones with peach undertones or sheer glosses.

Make your own!

Apricot and Lemon Lip Balm

Melt one teaspoon beeswax in a pot. Add one teaspoon apricot kernel oil and one teaspoon calendula oil (available at health food stores). Stir constantly. Remove from heat while stirring and add a few drops of lemon or orange essential oil. Store in a small glass pot.

Blushing Beauty

Know that great, healthy look you have when you first come out of the

shower or in from a soccer match? Healthy, well-rested skin usually has a natural glow to it. But there's nothing wrong with trying to enhance it a little!

Blushes pretty much come in three forms: powder, cream, or gel. If you have oily skin consider creams or gels . . . they're longer-lasting and won't streak like powders. Plus, creams and gels tend to give a more natural "just pinched my cheeks" look. In fact, to choose the best color for you, try pinching the apples of your cheeks. The natural flush of color that comes to your cheeks is the color to try to match!

For the most natural look, apply just a spot of cream or gel blush to your fingertip and dab a dot on each "apple," rubbing outward toward your temples. Overdid it? Dot on a little concealer or powder over it to minimize the color.

For powder blushes, use a big brush and lightly dust the color over the apple of your cheeks, brushing outward across your cheeks toward your temples.

103

In a pinch and without any blush? Use a dot of lipstick instead! Place a dab on each cheek and rub in just as you would a cream or gel blush!

For That Party Look!

Glitter is a great way to add a little pizazz to your look! And here's a recipe to make your own custom glitter!

Quarter cup aloe vera gel
One teaspoon baby oil
Three teaspoons fine polyester glitter (pick your own color — available at craft stores)

Mix all of the ingredients together! If you want to get really fancy, add a little of your favorite perfume! Apply a little glitter to your shoulders, cheeks, and legs for a fun party look!

You can even package it for your friends and give it as gifts!

Nail It!

Longing for nice-looking nails? Here's how to give yourself your own salon-style manicure at home!

You need:

Nail polish remover (acetone free)

Cotton balls

Orange stick

Emery board

Nail brush

Hand cream

Base coat

Nail polish

Top coat

(All of the above are available at your local drugstore.)

Bowl of warm, soapy water

Two washcloths

1. Remove old nail polish by soaking a cotton ball with remover and holding it on your nail for about ten seconds. (You may need three or four cotton balls.)

2. Using the emery board (never use a file — it rips nails!), file your nails in one direction . . . be gentle! Angle your emery board slightly under the nail. File into desired shape . . . a squared-off oval is always a good look.

3. Soak your hands in warm, sudsy water for a few minutes to soften the cuticle (the white line at the base of your nails).

4. Use a clean nailbrush to remove any dirt under the nails.

5. Dampen the washcloths with hot water (as hot as your hands can stand). Massage some hand cream into your hands and nails and wrap a washcloth around each hand. Leave on for one minute.

6. Using the orange stick, gently push back your cuticle toward the nail base, so it's even.

7. Apply base coat to protect the nail from discoloration and prepare the surface for an even coat of polish.

8. Apply two coats of polish (wait four minutes in between), keeping the coats as thin as possible! Start at the base of the center of the nail and use three strokes to cover the entire nail (middle, left side, right side).

9. Apply a top coat once nails are completely dry.

Store nail polish in the fridge to keep it from getting clumpy. Too late? Add a drop or two of remover to the bottle and roll the bottle back and forth between your hands.

Never shake a nail polish bottle to mix . . . you'll get bubbles in the polish and on your nails! Roll it between your hands or on a table instead.

Q. As soon as I do my nails, I smudge one . . . help!

A. Who hasn't had this happen?! There's an easy solution: Put a drop of nail polish remover on your finger (careful!) and lightly smooth over the smudge. Let dry, and put on a fresh coat of color.

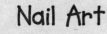

Nail Art

Want to add a little excitement to those newly polished nails? Here's how to create some flower power or perfect polka dots! All you need is a few fun colors of polish and some toothpicks. After your base coat has dried, dip one end of the tooth-pick into the color of your choice and simply dot on the nail. For a daisy pattern, surround a yellow dot with a circle of white dots!

Chapter 4
Sniff it Out!

Looking to make a statement? Fragrance is a fabulous way to do it! Have you ever gotten a whiff of a particular scent and been transported back to another time or place? Scents have the magical ability to evoke a whole range of feelings, moods, and memories. The good news is that there's no reason to spend a year's allowance to find that special scent. You can get your hands on all kinds of sweet-smelling (and affordable!) perfumes

and colognes at department stores and drugstores
. . . or you can try making your own out of essential oils (see page 115)!

Did you know that fragrances can be used for the
following benefits?

To improve your mood

To relax

*To increase efficiency and
alertness (try spritzing some
perfume on your wrist before
your next big test — take a
couple of whiffs to see if it works!)*

Select a fragrance that suits you! While
some like to vary their perfumes,
others prefer to select a "signature"
fragrance that becomes a part of who
they are!

Sniff it out!

Check out the quiz below to find out your perfume personality!

1. When you choose a book to read, you usually go for:

a) A tearjerker — who doesn't love a good cry?

b) An exotic mystery set in some faraway location.

c) Read? Who has time to read? You'd rather be outdoors kayaking, running, or hiking a mountain!

2. When you think of your dream date, it's:

a) Checking out the latest romantic comedy at the movies.

b) Trying a new Indian or Thai restaurant.

c) Going Rollerblading together.

3. You're going to your cousin's wedding and need to get an outfit. You choose:

a) A simple sundress.

b) A long, flowing ethnic print skirt and tank top.

c) A classic tailored dress.

4. If you could visit one place in the world, it would be:

a) Any quaint seaside village.

b) Bora Bora (need I say more?).

c) Colorado, without a doubt!

5. If you had to choose between the following flowers, you'd go for:

a) A pink rose.

b) An exotic tiger lily.

c) A daisy or sunflower.

6. If you were on a desert island and could only have one CD, it would be:

a) A collection of 'N Sync's love ballads.

b) Anything Latino! *Olé!*

c) Your nature sounds CD, naturally!

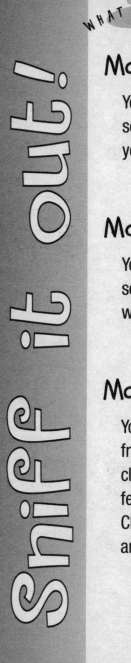

Sniff it out!

Mostly A's — Flower Girl

You're a romantic at heart! Choose something light and floral to accent your personality!

Mostly B's — Spice Girl

You're an adventurous, mysterious soul! Choose an exotic, spicy scent with warm tones.

Mostly C's — Nature Girl

You love the outdoors and anything fresh and natural! You need a clean, light scent that doesn't interfere with your active lifestyle. Choose something fruit-based, like an energizing citrus scent!

Testing Tips:

Ask cosmetic counters or beauty super-stores for samples to try at home.

When testing perfume make sure you're scent-free to start.

Only try one perfume on one part of your body.

Wait half an hour after spraying to get an accurate scent . . . it needs to set into your skin!

Fragrance Recipe
Refreshing Citrus Scent

One tablespoon mandarin oil

Four cups ethyl alcohol (available at drugstores)

One teaspoon lemon oil

Mix the mandarin oil with one cup of the alcohol until blended. Add the remaining alcohol and stir. Finally, stir in the lemon oil. Put in an airtight bottle or container for four to six weeks for it to reach its scentsational peak!

Spray your favorite fragrance on your curtains and bedding for an all-around scentsation!

Q. I absolutely love my best friend's perfume . . . but how come when I tried it on myself, it smelled totally different?

A. It's all chemistry! Everyone has a different skin chemistry, which is affected by diet, medication, natural skin oils, mood, and environmental factors. The way your normal fragrance smells can even change with changes in diets, medications, and climates! Your best bet is to test a fragrance on yourself . . . and stay in the same hemisphere!

Wear fragrance on the hottest parts of the body for the best scent (chest, wrists, behind the knees).

Storing Your Scents

Make sure to keep your perfumes and cologne away from direct sunlight and heat . . . otherwise you may end up with a funky twist to your normal scent!

Be careful not to spray perfume or cologne on your clothing . . . it can stain! Too late? Dab the stain with soda water and rinse before washing as normal.

Put a couple drops of perfume or essential oil in your shampoo for sweet-smelling hair!

Chapter 5
Closet Emergency!

The great thing about fashion in the new millennium is that there are no rules! It can be anything you want it to be. Sure, certain trends will still come and go (please, no more bell-bottoms!), but never before have girls been so free to create their own look.

How Do You Choose Your Own Look?

It's really pretty easy. You'll find that when you go shopping there are certain things you like and certain things that you wouldn't be caught wearing even alone in your room! Trust your instincts

and try not to "buy into" that leopard-print skirt just because it's hip. It'll probably stay in your closet with the tags still on!

Clothes Control

So you're out shopping and you see this fabulous, retro-style shirt that you absolutely cannot live without. Before you run to buy it . . . stop! When you're out shopping it's good to keep in mind the other things you have in your closet. Do you have a skirt or bottoms that will match the top? Will you have to go looking for something to wear with it? Sometimes buying one thing "you can't live without" means having to buy something else that you otherwise wouldn't have!

Avoid impulse buying! If you love something and think you want it, need it, have to have it that second – wait! Step back, take a walk, and come back twenty minutes later. If you're still that excited and it's in budget . . . go for it!

✳ Figure out what colors look best on you (ask your mother or a friend for help if you need to). Try buying things in that color scheme to look great . . . and make matching easier!

Gretchen's Rule

See something in a catalog that you **MUST** have . . . but it's totally over budget? Tear it out and stick it on the wall next to your bed. After about a month, the excitement will wear off and it'll be the last thing on your list!

Remember how excited you were the moment you bought that awesome skirt a couple of months ago? Well, it still looks as good as the first time you wore it. Try to remember that excitement the fifth, sixth, and sixtieth time you wear it ... and you won't go broke!

Retail Alternatives

Remember that pillow you made in sewing class? Well, a sewing machine and a little creativity can go a long way. There was a time when homemade clothes meant polyester pants ... but no more! Now you can pick out groovy patterns (*Vogue* even makes them ... check out your local fabric shop) and the fabric of your choice for a custom look. Talk about totally expressing yourself!

Not So Craftily Inclined?
Thrifty Thrift Shops

Check out the thrift shops! For real? Yes! If models can do it ... why not you?! Grab a girlfriend and have some fun! You can guarantee no one in school will have the same outfit!

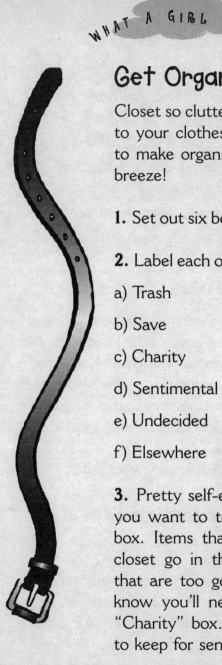

Get Organized!

Closet so cluttered you can't even get to your clothes? Here are some tips to make organizing your wardrobe a breeze!

1. Set out six boxes.

2. Label each of the boxes

a) Trash

b) Save

c) Charity

d) Sentimental

e) Undecided

f) Elsewhere

3. Pretty self-explanatory . . . Items you want to toss go in the "Trash" box. Items that will return to your closet go in the "Save" box. Items that are too good to trash, but you know you'll never wear, put in the "Charity" box. Items that you want to keep for sentimental reasons go in

"Sentimental" box. No idea where to put something? Toss it in the "Undecided" box. If something belongs somewhere else and just ended up in your closet by default, put it in the "Elsewhere" box.

4. Now just do as the boxes say! Throw out the "Trash" box. Hang up the "Save" box items in your closet. Bring the "Charity" box to a charity shop. Store your "Sentimental" box under the bed so you can take a look at the items every once in a while without them being in your way. Make a decision about the "Undecided" and put the "Elsewhere" items back where they belong!

S-o-r-t-e-d!

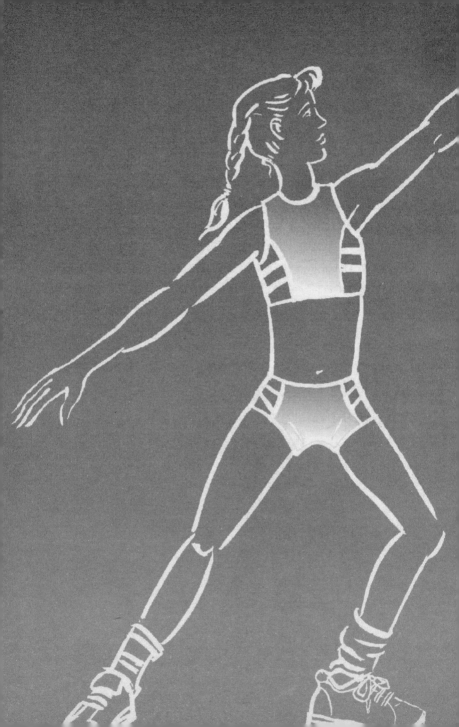

PART 3

HEALTH & HAPPINESS

Chapter 1
Shape Up!

Nothing feels better inside and out than being in good shape! Your skin glows, your hair shines, you feel strong, empowered . . . the best you can be! And being in shape doesn't mean running a marathon or even playing a team sport. It means moving around and having a good time anyway you can . . . whether it's dancing around the living room, Rollerblading around the block, shooting hoops, or doing yoga! Not sure what sport is best for you? Find out your workout personality below!

In order to get into a routine that you'll enjoy and keep at,

you need to figure out what activities best match your schedule, interests, and personality. Once you figure out your fitness style, you can choose a workout that you actually enjoy!

1. If you could pick your ultimate workout goal, it would be:

(a) To complete a marathon or triathlon.

(b) To be a member of an Olympic team.

(c) To be an extreme-sport star.

2. When it comes to working out, you:

(a) Are totally self-disciplined and have no problem working out alone.

(b) Have to work out with friends or teammates to stay energized.

(c) Need constant challenges — you like to try a ton of new things.

3. Do you like sports because:

(a) They give you a chance to focus on your body and reflect on your goals?

(b) They give you a sense of belonging?

(c) It's a good way to add variety to your day?

4. You are biking with a friend who's having a tough time keeping up. You think:

(a) I wish she wasn't holding me back.

(b) No big deal. At least we're having a good time.

(c) Let's find something else to do!

5. When it comes to trying a new exercise, you:

(a) Feel like you can't let up until you perfect it.

(b) Think of it as a chance to have fun with some friends.

(c) Look at it as an opportunity to learn something you've never tried before.

If you answered mostly A's, you're better off exercising on your own. Your best workouts are ones that require concentration and focus on your body and mind.

Sports that may be to your liking include cycling, swimming, jogging, surfing, and rock climbing.

If you answered mostly B's, when it comes to exercise your focus is on **FUN**! Your friends always give you that little extra, especially when you're sweating through a workout together. Go for group activities like aerobics, basketball, volleyball, softball, or kickboxing.

If you answered mostly C's, your feeling on exercise is "change it up"! None of the same old, same old workouts for you! You need a constantly changing routine to keep you interested and motivated! Try mixing it up with some mountain biking, fencing, windsurfing, kayaking, or snowboarding.

Before beginning any type of exercise, it's important to warm your body up . . . otherwise you run the risk of pulling a muscle, straining a ligament, or having some other painful injury!

Warming Up/Cooling Down

Warming up is an important part of exercise! It does just what it says — warms up your muscles to help you avoid injury. Before you launch into your routine, try jogging in place or doing a few sets of jumping jacks to get your body ready!

Cooling down is pretty much the flip side of warming up . . . and just as important. After finishing your workout, make sure you stretch, stretch, stretch! This will help prevent sore and stiff muscles . . . and make it lots easier to go up and down stairs the next day!

When doing any kind of aerobic exercise, breathe! Your muscles need oxygen to work and grow!

Exercise in Disguise!

To get the benefits of exercise, you don't necessarily have to go for a twenty-mile bike ride or do an hour of exercise videos. Exercise is cumulative, which means that doing a little bit a few times a day is just as effective as doing a longer session once a day! Here are a few not-so-traditional ways to get your heart pumping and that bod moving!

Dancing. Have a dance party on your own, or invite a few friends over.

Vacuuming. Your parents are sure to love this one! Vacuum the whole house and burn off a couple of those chocolate chip cookies!

Walk it! Instead of getting a ride, why not try walking there?

Take the stairs. Get into the habit of taking the stairs instead of an elevator or escalator. Just a little bit each day will help build stronger legs and a stronger heart!

Mowing the lawn. A great cardio workout — especially for bigger lawns! (Doesn't quite work if you have a seated mower!)

✱ Don't have dumbbells? Use canned food from the pantry!

At Home Workout

Don't belong to a gym? No worries! You can get a gym-quality workout at home . . . no equipment necessary!

Ab Firmer

Sit on the floor, knees up and ankles crossed. Place arms by your side, palms down for balance. Lift feet a few inches off the ground and rock forward while simultaneously raising your knees toward your shoulders. Hold for a second, then return to starting position. Try to work up to three sets of eight repetitions each.

Butt and Thigh Blaster

Stand with feet shoulder width apart. Raise arms straight over head and press palms together, elbows by your ears. Lower into a squat by pushing hips back and bending knees, keeping knees over ankles.

Reach right leg back as far as you can and lower hips slightly to lunge. Squeeze left buttocks to

return to a standing position, legs straight. Squat again and lunge back with left leg. Hold abs tight throughout to keep upper body stable. Repeat six times on each leg.

Upper Body Builder

Start on hands and knees, back flat. Extend right leg out in back, toes pointed. Inhale and bend elbows to lower your chest toward the ground. Exhale and push hands down to straighten arms and raise upper body. Switch legs and repeat. Do twelve push-ups, alternating legs.

Chapter 2
Nutrition

Figuring out what food to eat is no easy task! You can read something in a mag that says one thing, then hear something totally different on TV, and something else from your parents! Well, the good news is that eating healthy does not mean completely giving up those double-chocolate brownies and yummy potato chips. It's about making choices from a wide variety of foods . . . and the amounts of those foods that you consume! The better your choices are, the healthier you'll feel inside and out!

You are what you eat! From the second that you bite down on that first tasty morsel, your food is being turned into fuel that will move from your stomach into your intestines and be reabsorbed into your body.

The nutrients are what power your body! Foods like apples, brown rice, eggs, and spinach are rich in nutrients like carbohydrates, protein, and necessary fats. You need all these nutrients to stay healthy and happy!

Carbohydrates

The energy provider! Healthy carbs, including fruits and vegetables, will keep your body running at a constant level. Refined carbs like processed (white) flours, candies, sugar cereals, white sugar, cakes, and cookies will give you a quick jolt of energy but leave you lacking afterward. These should not be a foundation for your daily diet.

Proteins

Proteins provide the building materials your body needs to make and repair muscles, organs, bones, and more! Protein comes from meat, poultry, and fish as well as dairy products like eggs, cheese and milk, and nuts, too!

Fats

Fats are the body's backup fuel system and are important for maintaining healthy hair, skin, and nails. Everyone needs fat in their diets, but because fat is stored (for women, most typically on their thighs, butts, and tummies) for tougher times, it's best to eat it in moderation. There are basically two types of fat: unsaturated and saturated. Unsaturated fats usually come in liquid form and include olive oil, sunflower oil, canola oil, corn oil, plus seed oils like sesame seed and peanut oils. These are generally better for you than saturated fats, which come in solid form and include things like lard and butter.

You Need Fat to Be Fit!

Fat is totally normal, not to mention necessary, for good health. You pretty much aren't fit if you don't have enough body fat.

My parents never buy junk food – you know, sugar cereals, chips, cookies, that kind of stuff. It used to bother me when my friends would come over and all we had was fruit. But now I don't even like stuff that's bad for me. I feel so much better putting healthy things in my body!

CASSIE, 12

Eat more, lose weight, feel great! Sound like the cover of some gimmicky weight loss program? Well, if you eat the right foods . . . it can be true. Junk foods like chips, cookies, pastries, and fried anything can fill you up, are hard for your body to burn off, and can leave you feeling pretty icky inside and out. Instead, you can eat more of the kinds of foods that are good for you, like fruits, vegetables, lean meats, and whole grains, and maintain your body's ideal weight and energy levels. The word "diet" doesn't even need to be in your vocab! It's all about making healthy choices about what you eat, not denying yourself food! If you make those choices smartly you'll feel and look good inside and out!

A good guideline?
Try to

choose foods that you could find or are made of things that you could find in nature. This means plenty of fruits and veggies, fish, meat, poultry, and whole grains. Try to avoid foods that are processed or contain chemicals and preservatives that you've never heard of.

Three Meals a Day . . . at Least!

You should never, ever, ever skip meals, especially breakfast! You need a healthy fix in the morning to give you energy to get you through the day. Don't have time for a complete breakfast buffet? At least grab a banana, yogurt, or piece of whole grain toast with peanut butter as you run for the bus! Skipping meals slows down your metabolism and makes it harder for your body to work properly (including the burning of fat!). So if you think you're going to lose weight by skipping meals, think again! Your best bet is to have at least three medium meals or, even better, five smaller meals throughout the day. Your body works best this way!

Eating well doesn't equal tasting bad. Here are a few tasty recipes sure to make your tummy happy!

Strawberry-Almond Smoothie

(in only five minutes!)

You'll need:

One cup strawberry yogurt
Two cups cleaned and halved strawberries
One small banana, sliced
One tablespoon honey
Two tablespoons sliced almonds
One cup vanilla soy milk (optional)

Place all the ingredients in the blender or food processor and blend until smooth (about two minutes). Pour into a tall glass and enjoy!

Veggie Power Salad

Two cups mixed salad greens
Half cup chopped ripe
    tomato
Half cup chopped yellow
    pepper

            Half cup cauliflower
                or broccoli florets
            Three thin slices of avocado
            Third cup canned kidney beans

Combine all ingredients in a large salad bowl and toss with the healthy blue cheese dressing on the next page.

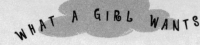

Dressing

One cup low-fat cottage
cheese
One cup plain nonfat yogurt
One teaspoon dried parsley
One teaspoon lemon juice
Half teaspoon Worcestershire
sauce
Pinch of black pepper
Third of a cup of fresh blue cheese

Blend all the ingredients except cheese in a blender.
Crumble blue cheese into mixture and stir.

Tasty Chicken Pot Stickers

You'll need:
One pound ground chicken breast
Two tablespoons reduced-sodium soy sauce
Salt and black pepper to taste
Third cup chopped green onions
One tablespoon sesame oil
Half cup reduced-sodium, nonfat chicken broth
Eight 6" square egg-roll wrappers

Combine the first four ingredients in a large bowl. Mix well and divide into eight equal portions. Place each portion on the center of a wrapper. Moisten wrapper edges with water and pull up corners to meet in center. Pinch together edges to seal. Heat oil in large nonstick skillet over medium heat. Sauté the pot stickers, flat side down, for two minutes, or until golden brown on the bottom. Add broth, cover, and steam for five minutes. Serve soy sauce on the side.

Snack It!

The word "snack" doesn't have to mean junk food! There are plenty of healthy, yummy-tasting treats to get you through to your next meal. Try one of these.

All-natural yogurt with wheat germ or granola sprinkled on top

Almonds (unsalted) mixed with dried cranberries

Apple wedges with all-natural peanut butter

Bon appétit!

Chapter 3
The Stress Mess

You've got an oral report due tomorrow, the coach has asked you to star in the big game, your mother won't let you go to the biggest party of the year because you forgot to take out the trash . . . your hands are sweaty, your heart's beating faster, you can't think straight . . . what's going on? You're stressed!

 Deep breathing can help calm you down. Inhale slowly and hold the breath for a second, then slowly exhale. As you exhale, try to relax your shoulders.

Believe it or not, stress is a totally normal feeling. It's unavoidable. Everyone experiences it! It's your body's natural instinct to protect itself from emotional or physical pressure. Some stress helps you get things done. It can help us finish projects, study for a test, do well in sports, music, dance. But too much stress can drive you nuts!

So what causes stress? Stress can be caused by lots of things: body changes, expectations from your teachers or parents, peer pressures, communication problems with friends and parents, or family breakups.

Signs You're Stressed:

Feeling depressed or tired much of the time.

Having trouble sleeping.

Crying for no reason.

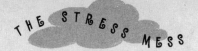
Blaming other people for things that happen to you.

Only seeing the downside of a situation.

Having headaches and stomachaches.

How Can I Deal with Stress?

There are definitely things you can do to help relieve stress.

Exercising, eating healthy, and getting enough sleep get your body and mind in the condition they need to be in to face the world. Make sure you're getting enough!

Make a list of what's causing your stress. Is it friends? Family? School? Sports? A big concert coming up?

Take control of what you can. For example, if you have a big test coming up, don't wait until the last minute to study. Or try getting a study partner!

Give yourself a break. Remember that you can't make everyone in your life happy all the time. It's OK to make mistakes, learn from them, then let 'em go!

Don't commit yourself to things you can't or don't

want to do. If you're already too busy getting ready for the big game, don't promise to baby-sit for your neighbor. And most important . . . find someone to talk to! Talking to friends or family can help by giving you a chance to express your feelings. You might be surprised to find out how many people around you experience similar stress. If you don't feel like you can talk to a friend or family member, see a school counselor or church member. The most important thing is not to keep the stress inside!

Take a time-out . . . Spend a night reading a mag, sipping on some herbal tea, listening to some relaxing tunes, doing your nails, taking a bath . . . whatever you enjoy!

Yoga

Yoga is a fantastic all-around exercise for anyone! It can improve your posture, mood (great for de-stressing), circulation (which helps out the skin), and more. Here are a couple of moves to get you started!

The Child's Pose is great for beginners (and a super way to help release that pretest nervousness!).

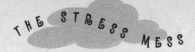

Get on all fours.

Lean back and sit on your knees.

Stretch your arms straight out in front of you as far as they can go.

Hold for a few minutes . . . or as long as you can.

You know all those headstands that you do just for fun with your friends? They're actually a yoga move! Here's an easier version that you can practice.

Lie on your back, feet straight out in front of you.

Lift your legs and backside up in the air, supporting your back with your arms.

Raise your legs straight above you as high as they can go and hold for as long as you can!

Alternate-nostril breathing is a quick and easy way to calm yourself down before a big game, test, or any other semi-nerve-racking event! Hold one nostril closed with your finger and inhale slowly and deeply with the other nostril, then exhale. Repeat with the other nostril.

Relaxing Herb Pillow

Looking for a gift that you can make for a friend? Or a treat to help you relax? Try making a relaxation pillow! You can pick up dried herbs at nature or health food shops, online, or at select gift shops. The best kinds for relaxation are lavender, chamomile, and peppermint. Just cut two squares (or another shape of choice) of fabric approximately the size of the pillow you'd like to make. Sew along the edges, leaving a space about two inches long. Pour the herbs (try mixing them) into the space. Fit as much as you can, then stitch up the space by hand. You can also decorate the pillow with ribbon, button, beads . . . be creative!

Stress-B-Gone Bath Blend

Add the following to your bath for a truly relaxing experience.

Fifteen drops lavender oil

Twenty drops mandarin oil

One teaspoon sunflower, almond, or apricot kernel oil

Putting it all

ogether

So now you've got great hair, good skin, fun friends, and you are getting along with your sister or brother! Most important, you have the confidence to get out and make your mark in this crazy, exciting, ever-changing, never ever boring world! And if once in a while you have a temporary case of "I don't feel so great about myself" due to a zit in the wrong place at the wrong time or a fight with a friend . . . don't panic . . . it's normal! Now you have the crisis tools necessary to get through it!

Top 10 things to remember on your trip to teendom

1. You are AMAZING! Don't try to be someone else . . . make the most of the incredible person YOU are!

2. It's great to look and feel good on the outside, but a thousand times better if you're good on the inside.

3. Be nice to EVERYONE.

4. Don't pick your zits.

5. Drink lots of water.

6. Get lots of sleep.

7. If you have a choice between a cake or an apple . . . go for the apple!

8. Find a sport or exercise that you love and do it as much as you can.

9. You have only one family . . . try to get along!

10. Choose your friends wisely.

As you head toward the teens, you're learning and discovering all kinds of amazing things about yourself and the world around you. Believe it or not, every experience (good and bad) will help you learn about who you are — and who you aren't. The most important thing to remember? It's all about being true to you! So put on that smile, drink some water, and celebrate the one thing you're better at than anyone else in the world . . . being you, and I'll guarantee you'll have a "heavenly" trip!